IRISH LIFE AND CULTURE

XVI

THE IRISH HARP

CLÁIRSEACH NA hÉIREANN

JOAN RIMMER

Arna chur amach do Chomhar Cultúra Éireann
ag Cló Mercier, 4 Sráid an Droichid, Corcaigh

THE IRISH HARP

JOAN RIMMER

Published for the Cultural Relations Committee by
The Mercier Press, 4 Bridge Street, Cork.

© THE GOVERNMENT OF IRELAND

ISBN 0 85342 151 X
FIRST EDITION 1969
SECOND EDITION 1977

THE aim of this series is to give a broad, informed survey of Irish life and culture, past and present. Each writer is left free to deal with his subject in his own way, and the views expressed are not necessarily those of the Committee. The general editor of the series is Caoimhín Ó Danachair.

Joan Rimmer is a free-lance writer and broadcaster on musical subjects, author of specialist studies on the morphology of the Irish Harp and the Triple Harp, of *Musical Instruments of Ancient Western Asia* (British Museum publication) of twelve articles in the sixth edition of *Grove's Dictionary of Music and Musicians* and with her husband Frank Harrison, of *European Musical Instruments* and a number of articles on ethnomusicological subjects.

PRINTED IN THE REPUBLIC OF IRELAND BY
RICHVIEW BROWNE & NOLAN LIMITED, DUBLIN

Contents

List of Plates

Foreword

SINCE 1967, when the text of this booklet was written, the scope and depth of Irish historical studies has expanded greatly in many areas, as have archaeological, linguistic and musical studies in western Asia in matters relevant to Ireland. There is considerably more evidence about early frame harps in western Europe, and certain aspects of music in Ireland are now the subject of disciplined investigation by some Irish scholars. However, little further concrete and factual information about the kind of harp that came to be known as Irish has come to light in the past decade and no further instruments of that type have been discovered. Apart from the final sentence and revision necessitated by re-assessment of the Sutton Hoo fragments, the text of this edition remains that of the first, as does its purpose in providing a general survey of Irish harps and their uses, for interested but not necessarily musical or organologically inclined readers.

Thanks are due to the people and institutions whose names appear in the list of acknowledgements. I also thank particularly Dr Liam O'Sullivan, formerly Keeper of the Arts and Industrial Division of the National Museum of Ireland, for invaluable help over several years, the private owners and museum curators who kindly allowed their instruments to be examined and photographed, Mrs. Mary Rowland for much patient research on techniques, Mr. Eric Halfpenny, Honorary Editor of the Journal of the Galpin Society, for encouragement during the earlier stages of research and the British Academy for a research grant which sustained part of it. I am also greatly indebted to Professor Brian Ó Cuiv, of the Dublin Institute for Advanced Studies, for advice and assistance with Irish texts, to Miss Maura Scannell, Assistant Keeper of the Natural History Division of the National Museum of Ireland, and Dr. Hayes, of Edinburgh University Forestry Department, for wood identifications, and to Professor James Tierney, University College, Dublin and Mr. Séamus Dalton of the translation department of Dáil Éireann for translations of the Latin and Irish inscriptions on the Dalway Fragments.

joan Rimmer

1. *The form of the Irish harp*

THE harp which is the emblem of Ireland and is depicted on her coinage is a real one, now preserved in Trinity College, Dublin. It is one of the very few European musical instruments which have survived more or less complete from medieval times, and when it was made, probably some time in the fourteenth century, it was already a recognisably Irish kind of harp. This was the characteristic instrument of Ireland for at least six centuries and by fortunate chance, no less than fourteen harps and fragments have survived, some from every century from the fourteenth to the eighteenth. Naturally it changed in certain respects over so long a period, but its essential character remained the same, as did that of the Irish style of performance.

A number of characteristic features distinguished the Irish harp from all others. In general, it was very solidly and robustly constructed. Most fundamental were the size and nature of the soundbox. Until the eighteenth century this was always made from one solid piece of willow, hollowed to form a deep 'box' whose walls were up to half an inch (1.3 cm.) thick. The open back was covered by a separate piece of different wood. There was a solid protuberance, or 'foot', at the base, on which the harp rested. Only two other objects are always made of willow—the cricket bat and the old-fashioned one-piece clothes peg. Both are dependent for efficiency on the physical properties of willow-wood, on its unusual combination of strength and resilience, and these must have been the qualities which made it perfect for the soundboxes of the great Irish harps. The forepillar ('bow' in old terminology) was thick; it curved outwards and was generally T-shaped in section, with the stem of the T on the inner side and the broad part facing forwards. The neck was deep and heavy and was reinforced with metal bands on both sides. Metal pins set low in the neck through the reinforcing bands, carried the strings on the left side. The lower ends of the strings were twisted round wooden toggles inside the box. A horse-shoe-shaped metal loop was rivetted to the box round the upper half of each string hole.

I

The strings were of thick brass, and they were plucked with long
fingernails, not with the flesh of the fingertips. The harp was held
on the left shoulder, the left hand playing in the upper register and
the right hand in the bass. All surviving Irish harps carry clear
wear-marks from this playing position, which was also that of old
Welsh harps but is not used for any other harps.

The reason seems clear from the nature of the early Irish harp.
A modern harp neck is cut away at one side of the treble end so
that the strings may run as nearly as possible in the same plane
throughout the harp. The medieval Irish harp's neck is set centrally
on the box; the highest strings, which are very short, are not only
right out of plane but are also out of parallel with each other and
are splayed into a fan shape. They are perfectly manageable with
the left hand if the harp rests on the left shoulder. If it rests on the
right, they are extremely awkward for the left hand and impossible
for the right, which must reach across the considerable width of
the neck in order to get to them at all. This position, though no
longer physically necessary on an instrument as large as the Irish
harp eventually became, was in fact used to the very end.

Irish harps can be classified into three kinds, each associated with
a definite period. That of the fourteenth, fifteenth and early sixteenth
centuries, and perhaps of the thirteenth also, though we have no
concrete evidence about this, was about two feet four inches
(70 cm.) high. The forepillar was mortised into the heavy neck
which overhung it, the soundbox was of the same depth all
through and there were about thirty strings. Three examples of
this type, the *small low-headed Irish harp*, are extant (Plates 11, 12,
13). The typical instrument of the late sixteenth and of the seventeenth century was the *large low-headed Irish harp* (Plates 17–27),
essentially the same instrument in bigger size with more strings
and a soundbox which increased in depth as it narrowed in width
towards the treble. There are four complete harps and two sets
of fragments of this type. The final form, made in the eighteenth
century, was the *high-headed Irish harp* (Plates 30–34). In this,
the forepillar was almost straight and much taller than in the
large low-headed harps, though the instruments were not always
bigger otherwise. The neck swept upwards sharply to meet the top
of the forepillar, thus forming the 'high head', and the bass strings
were longer in relation to the others than was the case in the earlier
harps. Individual 'shoes of the strings' were replaced by a single

perforated metal strip down the middle of the belly. We have four true high-headed Irish harps and another which has some Irish characteristics.

Few of the artists who made romantic and often imaginary portraits of Irish harpers in the eighteenth and early nineteenth centuries observed and depicted exactly the form of those harpers' instruments, and we are fortunate in having so much evidence from the harps themselves. But stringed instruments were used in pre-Christian and early Christian Ireland long before any kind of harp is known to have existed in north-western Europe. How did the harp come to Ireland and how did a particular kind of harp evolve or survive there? We shall try to answer these questions in the succeeding chapters.

2. The Harps and Lyres of Antiquity

IN great civilizations music has as characteristic a form as social organization, clothes or food, and the instruments on which it is played are, or were before the era of mechanical reproduction and instant communication, equally characteristic. The pre-Hispanic societies of Mexico, for example, had flutes, drums, rattles and scrapers of great musical subtlety, but no stringed instruments. Harps were used in the two earliest known urban civilizations, the Sumerian and the ancient Egyptian, but in Greece and Rome, as in India and China, they were originally exotic foreign instruments. The harp as we know it today—a triangular instrument completely enclosed on all three sides—is a European development dating, in all probability, only from the early Middle Ages.

We know nothing about the remote origin of the harp and very little about the origin of the European harps including the Irish form. How is it that many of the earliest known representations of the frame-harp, as the European harp is called in instrument classification, came from Celtic or Celtic-influenced places? Why did Irish harpers, from the twelfth century onwards, have such a high reputation in Europe? Why was the Irish word for a harp *cruit*, which must originally have meant not a harp, but a lyre? How did a distinctive form of harp come to be retained for so long in Ireland? To answer these questions conclusively is difficult. In order to try and answer them even partially, we must look first at what is known of the musical practices and instruments of the ancient peoples of Western Asia and Eastern Europe, both civilized and barbarian, since it was from those directions that the ancestors of the Celtic peoples originally came.

Among the treasures which Sir Leonard Woolley found in the burial chambers at Ur in Mesopotamia, dating from the middle of the third millenium B.C., were the remains, varying from fragmentary to nearly complete, of nine lyres and three harps. The main difference between a lyre and a harp lies in the relative positions of strings and sound-box. A lyre is basically of quadrangular or modified quadrangular shape. It consists of a soundbox surmounted by two 'arms' which are connected with each other at the top by a 'yoke'. The strings are fixed at the bottom of the box and then run across it, generally, but not always, over a bridge; they are attached at the upper end to the yoke, that part of the string which is clear of the box being free on both sides. The string lengths do not vary greatly except in oblique lyres. A harp, with one exception which will be discussed later, is basically of triangular shape. It has a soundbox, a string-carrying member (in Asiatic harps more accurately called an 'arm', while in European harps it is called a 'neck') at an angle from the box, and, in the case of the frame harps, a third part, the forepillar, which runs between the end of the neck and the end of the soundbox, thus enclosing the strings in a solid frame. The strings are fixed at one end directly into the centre of the box and at the other to the string-carrying member. They are free on both sides throughout their whole length, which is different for each note.

The lyres found at Ur were all of the curious kind which seems to have been used only in Sumerian civilization. They are nearly all large and cumbersome, with up to eleven strings, rectangular boxes beautifully cased or decorated with gold, silver and semi-precious stones, and often with the bull heads which connect them with older neolithic religion. On the victory face of the 'Standard' found at Ur, two musicians, a player of a big, eleven-stringed lyre and a singer or declaimer, perform during a courtly banquet. This and other depictions, together with the existence of extended tales such as those about Gilgamesh suggest that singing or chanting with a stringed instrument was already an established practice in the third millennium B.C. The last western European performers in this *genre*, the Irish declaimers and harpers of the sixteenth century, were heirs not only to an insular tradition stretching back to pre-Christian Ireland, but to one whose roots lie in the earliest Bronze Age civilization.

The Ur harps were arched harps, bow-shaped, with horizontal sound-boxes. One must have had at least fifteen strings, another twelve. While the great bull-lyre was the instrument used in the religious rituals and courtly music of the Sumerians, the harp seems to have had less solemn associations, for it was frequently depicted in erotic and festive or ritual drinking scenes. This arched harp, of which slightly different forms were used in Egypt also during the second half of the third and the first half of the second millennium B.C., had no European descendants, and though it was formerly played to some extent in India, it survives now only in Burma, Afghanistan and certain parts of the northern half of Africa.

Many depictions of musical instruments of the second millennium B.C. have survived from Western Asia and the Eastern Mediterranean, and they suggest musical usages and influences somewhat different from those of old Sumer. The big lyres are no longer seen

PLATE I. *Assyrian vertical harp. Stone relief from Nineveh; 7th century* B.C.

and a harp with a vertical soundbox, for whose existence there is evidence already in the middle of the third millennium, seems to have become the most important stringed instrument. It became known later in some form to the Greeks and the Chinese, lasted well into the Christian era in the Middle East generally and until the seventeenth century in Persia, and, as we shall see later, possibly had some influence on the evolution or invention of the European harps. It consisted of an elongated, boat-shaped sound-box covered with a skin belly and a string-carrying arm which protruded from it at an angle of about sixty degrees. Early depictions show only six strings; the Assyrian vertical harps, of which Plate 1 shows an example from the seventh century B.C. depicted on a relief of Ashurbanipal II at Nineveh, had 18 or 20, while Persian seventeenth-century harps had as many as forty strings. It appears to the modern eye to be 'in reverse', for its box was held almost upright against the player's chest, while the string-carrier was horizontal and the strings were more or less vertical. There was also another variety, with sound-box and string-carrier at right angles to each other, whose earliest known depiction comes from Egypt of the mid-second millennium B.C., though it was not necessarily of Egyptian origin. A big, angled harp, strangely like the European harp but without a forepillar, appeared in Egypt towards the end of the second millennium B.C., but has no later ascertainable history. Another ancient western Asiatic form was the horizontal angled harp. The Assyrian variety (Plate 2) consisted of a box and string-carrier at right angles to each other; the box in this case, however, was horizontal and the string-carrier, which was carved in the form of a human arm with uplifted hand at the top, was vertical (Plate 2). Unlike all other harps, this was sounded with a plectrum, not with the fingers. It seems that unrequired notes were damped with the fingers of one hand while the other drew the plectrum across all the strings of which only the required notes sounded. This is related to some lyre techniques.

With the exception of this horizontal angled harp, varieties of which still exist in remote areas to the north of the old kingdom of Urartu (present-day Armenia), there is no reason to suppose that these instruments, which were sizeable and not very portable high art instruments of urban civilizations, impinged to any degree on the life of proto-Celtic or historic pre-Christian Celtic peoples. Their possible significance in the history of the Irish harp comes centuries later, when influences from their late forms may have reached Ireland through Christian sources. With the non-Sumerian lyres of the ancient world, however, the picture is very different. Certain lyres seem to have originated among barbarian peoples in Asia. The dispersal of some forms can be assumed, if not minutely traced, from the Black Sea to the Atlantic, and with them we come closer to the proto-Celtic peoples, to the historic Celts, and to the Celtic immigrants into Ireland whose language, society and in

PLATE 2. *Assyrian horizontal angled harp. Stone relief from Nineveh; 7th century* B.C.

many ways unique musical usages continued long after the old lyres were displaced by the harp.

Many forms of lyre were played by the peoples of the ancient world. Some can be readily identified with certain areas and civilizations. For example, horizontally-held oblique lyres seem to have been Western Semitic or Levantine in origin, whilst the tortoiseshell-bodied *lyra* and big wooden *kithara* were Greek. One kind of lyre, however, that which is basically U-shaped, with a rounded base, was known much earlier than any of these and was much more widely dispersed geographically. The oldest known depictions, dating from early in the second millennium B.C., are from Mesopotamia, and it is thought that this lyre, along with the lute, must have been introduced there by barbarian peoples from across the mountains of Iran. Certainly these lyres and lutes were small and portable instruments, unlike the bull-lyres of Sumer and the large harps of Babylon. The lyres of Crete and Mycenae were U-shaped also, and so were some of the Hittite lyres from Phrygia. Etruscan wall-paintings often show the later Greek instruments, but in scenes like the banquet in the world of the dead, in the Tomb of the Shields at Tarquinia, the ancient U-shaped lyre is played—a gentle musical reminder of the western Asiatic origin of the Etruscan people. The *phorminx*, Homer's lyre, must have been of this kind, for Greek representations before 700 B.C. show a U-shaped instrument.

We know something of the lyres used by these peoples of southwest Asia and the eastern Mediterranean because their civilizations were literate to some degree and were at least partly urban. Written references and painted and sculptured depictions have survived. But we know very little about the nomadic peoples amongst whom the small U-shaped lyre seems to have originated. Whatever archaeology has uncovered about the first Indo-Europeans in Eastern and Central Europe and the peoples of the Late Bronze or Early Iron Ages who may be considered Proto-Celts, it has as yet discovered little musical material. However, a number of European depictions of lyres from the seventh to the fourth centuries B.C. are known. Some are mere rectangles filled in with lines and suggest rather than depict instruments. Some are apparently round-based while others seem to be related in form and playing position to western Asiatic lyres known from the preceding millennium.

It seems likely that there were U-shaped lyres in the Celtic civilizations of Gaul in pre-Christian times. Some concrete evidence of these can be seen on the coins of Gaul. Gabrielle Fabre and Monique Moinjonet have written: 'Gaulish coins are the oldest artistic creations which, given the present state of proto-historic research, demonstrate the unity of Gaulish art and its regional diversity'. The use of coins in Gaul must be attributed in the first place to Greek influence, and many Greek symbols were used. The combination of a one- or two-horse chariot with a lyre, which appears on a number of Gaulish coins, must have had some Celtic significance, though we do not know what it was. On coins of the Sequani, whose territory towards the source of the Rhône-Saône must have had strong Greek influence from the third century B.C. onwards, the lyre is obviously the Greek *lyra*. This form also appears on coins of the Santones, from the coast near Bordeaux, of the Unelli and the Baiocasses, and of the Coriosolites, where it is associated with a single andro-cephalic horse. These last three tribes were in Armorica, that is, what is now Brittany and part of Normandy, an area even longer open to Mediterranean influences. It must be remembered, not only in this connection but also with reference to early Christian Ireland, that the ancient civilized world was held together largely by sea routes. The U-shaped lyre appears on coins of the Aedui and the Carnutes, whose territory lay in the north-east of what has been called 'La Grande Celtique'—the powerful central part of Gaul which was richest in iron and gold. The appearance of U-shaped lyres there cannot be explained by Greek influence, for instruments of this kind seem to have dropped out of use in Greece itself before the first Greek colonists settled in Gaul at the mouth of the Rhône, though they did survive through the Hellenistic period in parts of the Near East.

It seems highly probable that the characteristic stringed instrument of the Celts was a U-shaped lyre, originating, as did those of the Eastern Mediterranean peoples about whom we know much more, in South-west Asia. It seems, too, that the Celts may have preserved it in something not far removed from its original form, for a thousand years or so. This time span, which seems so great in an age of easy communication and rapid change, is not so great in terms of survival in ancient times. The cylindrical reed pipes of the ancient world, for example, had an ascertainable life-span in some form or other, of nearly three thousand years, and survive tenuously to this day.

What was the place of music in the life of those peoples of the ancient world for whom the lyre was the only stringed instrument? Literary sources, centuries apart in time and from opposite ends of Europe, give some picture of musical activity in societies earlier than and outside the complex commercial city civilizations of the Mediterranean. Though the written forms of the Homeric epics date only from the fifth century B.C. it is generally agreed that the oral epics from which they were derived were of about the eighth century B.C. and the events they describe happened at the end of the second millenium B.C., not so far distant in those times of slower cultural change. In the Iliad, music has great prestige and associations of power which are obvious in, for example, Hector's threat to Alexandros that 'the lyre will not avail you, nor all the gifts of Aphrodite'. The lyre was used in ritual music such as the lament for the death of summer, and Achilles amused himself by singing songs of the deeds of heroes with the lyre. In the Odyssey, however, we seem to be closer to the kind of situation which must have obtained in pre-Christian Ireland, with skilled professional musicians such as Demodocus, who was summoned formally by a herald when Alkinous wished to hear him sing and play the lyre. Certainly, lyre music was heard at every festive banquet, for Alkinous spoke of 'the lyre which is the mate of the rich banquet' and Odysseus commanded 'sport with dance and lyre, for they are the crown of the feast'.

Though the historic people whose exploits formed the basis of the Homeric epics were not Celtic, the structure of Celtic societies seems to have had much in common with theirs. Later European empire-builders noticed the indigenous music of other continents, when they noticed it at all, generally only in public places, and described it in European terms of reference. In just such a way the Greek and Roman writers who from the fourth century B.C. onwards described the Celts and some of their music, did so in quite other terms than the creators of the tales which we know in Homeric form alluded to the music of the old Greeks. Classical writers knew of the Celts in the first place as fighting men, either mercenaries or enemies. Polybius described the Celts at the battle of Telemon in 225 B.C. as vain and courageous and using trumpets in battle. Diodorus Siculus, who knew Southern Gaul at first hand, described in some detail Celtic methods of fighting. In James Tierney's translation it reads:

When the armies are drawn up in battle-array they are wont to advance before the battle-line and to challenge the bravest of their opponents to single combat . . . And when someone accepts their challenge to battle they loudly recite the deeds of valour of their ancestors and proclaim their own valorous quality, at the same time abusing and making little of their opponent and generally attempting to rob him beforehand of his fighting spirit . . . The blood-stained spoils they hand over to their attendants and carry off as booty, while striking up a paean and singing a song of victory.

Diodorus, however, also gave some information about other uses of music in Celtic society.

They are boasters and threateners and given to bombastic self-dramatization, and yet they are quick of mind and with a good natural ability for learning. They also have lyric poets whom they call Bards. They sing to the accompaniment of instruments resembling lyres, sometimes a eulogy and some-times a satire. They have also certain philosophers and theologians who are treated with special honour, whom they call Druids . . . Their custom is that no-one should offer sacrifice without a philosopher . . . And it is not only in the needs of peace but in war also that they carefully obey these men and their song-loving poets, and this is true not only of their friends but also of their enemies. For often times as armies approach each other in line of battle with their swords drawn and their spears raised for the charge, these men come forth between them and stop the conflict, as though they had spell-bound some kind of wild animals. Thus, even among the most savage barbarians anger yields to wisdom and Ares does homage to the Muses.

Some of the functions of music in these pre-Christian Celtic societies lasted in Ireland for nearly a thousand years. But the instrument we know in historic Ireland is the harp, not the lyre of the pre-Christian Celts. The time, place and circumstances in which the triangular frame harps, including the kind known later as the Irish harp, were evolved or invented, are by no means certain.

3. *The earliest frame harps and the Irish harp*

O N the iconographical evidence known at present, the fully-framed triangular harp appeared in the ninth century A.D. On surviving evidence, it was depicted occasionally in the ninth and tenth centuries, fairly frequently from the eleventh century onwards. On the whole, the accuracy of depiction in the eleventh and twelfth centuries seems to be related to some degree of Celtic or British or at any rate north-west European influence. The use of a bow on stringed instruments is traceable iconographically in the west from about the same date as the frame harp. Recent research has suggested that the bow's origin lay in western Asia. The pre-ninth-century history of the frame harp, however, is still a matter for speculation.

Depictions of musicians, chiefly David as King and Psalmist with his attendant players, abound in Christian iconography from the ninth century to the fourteenth. The stringed instruments played by David—all illustrating the Latin term *cithara*—include absurd and pseudo-antique conceptions of classical lyres, round Teutonic lyres, sometimes bowed, Western Asiatic psalteries and symbolic 'ten-stringed psalteries', harps and misconceptions of harps. The pre-medieval mixture of non-Christian with Western and·Eastern Christian tradition is nowhere more apparent than in musical representations.

The two basic characteristics which distinguish the shape of the frame harps of Europe from the open-fronted harps of the Eastern Mediterranean and Asia, that is, the presence of a forepillar and the position of the string-carrier above, not below the box, have already been mentioned; and two more, the nature of the box and the method of string-fixing and tuning, will be discussed later. While many early psalter illustrations and those from sources far removed from north-west Europe show harps lacking in, or with ill-defined forepillars, none shows harps of the Eastern kind with the soundbox uppermost.

The harps in psalters of the ninth century are quite small and completely triangular. A good example is in the Psalter called after Folchard, the scribe who made it some time in the third quarter of the ninth century for the library of the monastery of St. Gall (Plate 3). This monastery, which still houses some of the most precious of Irish manuscripts, was founded on the site of the cell of the Irish Saint Cellach, or Gallus in Latin. In the ninth century it was one of the greatest European centres of learning, and it was outstanding for the study of plainsong and for the production of liturgical manuscripts. Many elements are mixed in the decoration of Folchard's Psalter; there are Corinthian capitals, Irish spirals and convolutes and Carolingian plaitwork. The illustration of the return of the Ark of the Covenant shows a crowned David holding a tiny triangular harp whose soundbox and forepillar seem to be vestigial but whose tuning pins in the neck are very clearly defined.

Other early depictions of frame harps come from a geographically Celtic source—the sculptured stone crosses and cross-slabs of Scotland. Scholars disagree to some extent on the exact dating of many of these and of the Irish crosses also, but it is generally thought that the slabs and crosses sculptured with symbols, figure subjects and abstract decoration were made between the eighth and twelfth

PLATE 3. *David with small harp.* Psalter of Folchard; *9th century* A.D.

centuries. Both Scottish and Irish crosses contain a wealth of Celtic and non-Celtic symbols and motifs. It is possible that much of the material of early Eastern Christian iconography—crucifixion scenes, for example—was peculiarly alien to Celtic artists. The old testament story of David, however, surely cannot have been so, for it contains the glorification of heroic physical strength, in the rending of the lion's jaw and the slaying of Goliath, and the singing of joyful music with a stringed instrument. We know that both of these were a normal part of Celtic life.

On an upright cross slab at Nigg in Ross-shire, probably of the ninth or tenth century, there are armed men, animals, decorative patterns and symbols of David as strong man, shepherd and musician. He is shown in person slaying the lion and beside this scene is a horned sheep and a triangular harp with large soundbox, neck at right angles to it, a clearly-defined forepillar and seven strings. On the front of a cross at Dupplin in Perthshire, probably of later date, David rends the lion's jaw, while on the left side of the shaft is a seated figure playing a seven- or eight-stringed harp very similar to that on the Nigg stone. The rest of the Dupplin cross has, like the Nigg slab, warriors, birds, animals and decorative patterns. Two less accurately depicted harps are on fragments which have obvious Eastern Mediterranean influence and are probably of the eleventh or twelfth century. One, at Monifieth in Angus, shows a seated figure playing a seven- or eight-stringed harp with an absurdly thick neck and slender box and forepillar. On the same face is the lower part of a Byzantine-style crucifixion, with a straight-legged, tunicked Christ. One of the musician figures on a fragment at Ardchattan in Argyllshire has an odd harp with curved soundbox; it seems to be simply a Western Asiatic harp turned upside down. An upright cross-slab from Aldbar, in Angus, carries a now worn representation of an instrument which looks structurally closer to what we know as an Irish harp (Plate 4). On the back of the slab are two enthroned robed figures. Below them is a figure of David rending the lion's jaw, a staff, a harp, a horned sheep, a mounted man and a donkey-like animal. The harp has a thick soundbox, a curved forepillar, a neck which, although straight, appears slightly to overhang the forepillar; the stone is now too worn for certainty about the number of strings originally depicted.

It is difficult to date these crosses precisely and we know nothing at all of their makers except that they must have been hired by prosperous Christian communities or persons. But it is, perhaps, significant that three unequivocal depictions of harps at Nigg, Dupplin and Aldbar, all of which are in originally Pictish regions, are on crosses which carry, besides the David symbols, only hieratic and warrior figures, birds, beasts and decorative patterns, not crucifixions or overtly Christian symbols.

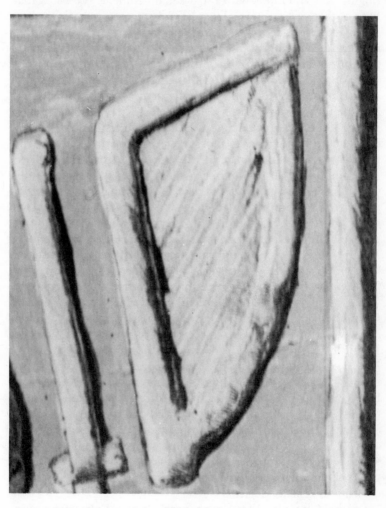

PLATE 4. *David's harp. Cross-slab from Aldbar; 11th–12th century(?)*

Since several of the Scottish crosses show harps, it would be reasonable to expect some evidence about Irish harps on the Irish crosses. Close examination of these, however, reveals the curious situation that, although they contain many more representations of stringed instruments than do the Scottish crosses, there are few which can be regarded as harps and no triangular frame harps at all. But the varieties of instruments, the possible provenance and

PLATE 5. *Seated figure with long round-topped lyre. Cross of the Scriptures, Clonmacnoise; 10th century*

the contexts in which they appear, provide some musical information from a time in Irish history about which we have very little
from other sources. The instruments on the Irish crosses are all
shown being played, not as isolated David symbols. Some of the
players are certainly David figures. That on the Carndonagh cross
plays a vaguely lyre-like instrument, now too worn for certain
identification. On the crosses at Killamery, Kinitty, and on the

PLATE 6. *The Last Judgement. Muiredeach's Cross, Monasterboice;* 10th
century

West Cross at Kells and the Cross of the Scriptures at Clonmacnoise (Plate 5) the instruments, although worn, all appear to be round-topped lyres. This kind of instrument is known from Anglo-Saxon manuscript sources from about the eighth century onwards and early medieval Germanic lyres were of a related shape. The musicians in the Last Judgment scenes on the east faces of the tenth-century Muiredeach's Cross at Monasterboice (Plate 6) may

PLATE 7. *The Last Judgement. Durrow Cross; 10th century*

have another significance, that of the Last Trump and the music of
the Blessed and the Damned. The latter is represented by a player of
triple pipes which seem, in some medieval iconography, to have
the same evil associations which double pipes had for the early
Christian Fathers. The instrument of the Blessed is an oblique lyre
on whose yoke a bird perches. This motif is of great antiquity and
can be traced back to the early second millennium B.C. in Mesopotamia. The lyre on the Durrow cross (Plate 7) is a curious instrument
with one straight and one curved arm. The oblique lyre of Muiredeach's cross appears also in the scene at the top of the east face of the
South Cross at Kells, which shows the miracle of the Loaves and
Fishes plus a lyre-playing figure at the left. This has generally been
assumed to be David, though the incongruity of his figure in this
scene has been admitted. It seems much more likely that it was not
intended to be David but that lyre-player without whom, as
Homer's Alkinous and Achilles and every early Irish king and
chieftain would have agreed, no feast was complete. The miracle,
after all, consisted of turning a few mouthfuls into food for a
multitude, a public feast.

The remaining stringed instruments on the Irish crosses, that is
on the South and North Crosses at Castledermot and one of the
Ullard crosses, all of about the ninth or tenth centuries, seem to be
harps, but they are of a type whose outline is nearly quadrangular.
Of these three the South Cross at Castledermot (Plate 8) is in the
best condition. It shows an instrument with a shallow horizontal
bar which is probably a soundbox, a curved 'arm' or 'neck'
(normal harp terminology is difficult to apply to this kind of harp)
which rises from one end of the box and overhangs it. A slender
forepillar joins the end of the overhanging curve to the other end
of the horizontal part. Fragments which were found in the Saxon
ship burial at Sutton Hoo, Suffolk, England, dating from the
seventh century A.D., were formerly thought to be this kind of
instrument. They are now known to be remains of a long lyre,
and have been thus re-assembled. No strings survived with the
Sutton Hoo fragments, but the 'neck' had remains of six pins,
and the three harps on the Irish crosses appear to have six strings.
They are played by isolated, seated figures, all on the left arm of the
crosses, and their context suggests that they may not be Davids.
The other scenes on the faces on which these harpers appear are
not, as with the lyres already discussed, parts of the David cycle or

Christ in Glory or the Last Judgment or miracles. They are mostly scenes of violence—the Crucifixion, the Fall, the Massacre of the Innocents, Jacob wrestling with the Angel. Moreover, they are on the west faces of the crosses, not on the east, as are the scenes of glory and triumph. We do not know the functions of this kind of quadrangular harp *c.* 900 A.D. If it had Viking associations for the Christian Irish, these harpers may perhaps represent not David, the psalmist and precursor of Christ, but the music of triumphant evil.

PLATE 8. *Seated figure with quadrangular harp. South Cross, Castledermot; 9th century*

Although we know nothing of the musical associations in the minds and ears of the sculptors of the high crosses, a few conclusions can be drawn, always bearing in mind that survival is so fortuitous that our evidence can only be partial. First, since there is no record of oblique lyres in western Europe, those which appear may have been taken from some near eastern source which showed already archaic lyres. Second, the round-topped lyres on some of the earlier Irish crosses may be examples of a solid, wooden-framed instrument which, possibly, some Celtic as well as Teutonic people used in the first seven or eight centuries of the Christian era. Third, while the triangular harp seems to have been ordinary enough in Scotland to receive clear treatment from some sculptors, it perhaps had associations which were not conventional Roman or Byzantine Christian; the subjects on Irish crosses are, on the whole, more doctrinally oriented than those on the Scottish crosses, and stronger conventions of what was or was not proper to show as a 'holy' instrument may have operated in Ireland. Triangular harps may have been used in Ireland at the very time when sculptors were still carefully depicting lyres; if we accept the late dating which some scholars propose for many of the Irish crosses, we can be fairly certain that they were.

In the earliest Irish manuscripts *cruit* is the word for a stringed instrument, and it continued to be used in Irish for what we call a harp. It is cognate with *crwth*, *chrotta*, *rota*, *rote*, etc., some of which we know to have been lyres, although *rota* and *rote* were later used ambiguously and in medieval times sometimes designated small harps. The word is derived from the Indo-European root KER— meaning bent or curved; the form KEREB is the root of the word *harp* whose first known reference is in an often-quoted poem by Venantius Fortunatus, who was Bishop of Poitiers in the sixth century A.D. He wrote a multitude of praise poems for the Frankish nobles among whom he spent much of his life, and this itself reflects a northern tradition, Teutonic or Celtic as much as Roman. In one set of poems in praise of Duke Lupus these lines occur:

> *Romanusque lyra, plaudat tibi barbarus harpa,*
> *Graecus Achilliaca, crotta Britanna canat.*

The Romans praise thee with the lyre, the barbarians with the harp,
The Greeks with the Achillean lyre, the Britons with the crotta.

What did Venantius Fortunatus mean by *harpa*? He knew Germania, that is, the Romanised Rhineland and its hinterland, at first hand, and it is probable that his 'barbarians' were Teutonic peoples beyond the Rhine. Nevertheless, we cannot tell whether *harpa* meant what we know as a harp or was simply the Teutonic word for a lyre. It seems, however, that to Venantius Fortunatus these four terms designated different instruments, even though they may, in fact, have been only distinguishable varieties of lyre.

There seem to be two possibilities about the development of the harp, not necessarily mutually exclusive and perhaps complementary. One is that some Teutonic peoples may have had a small angled harp, perhaps like those which still survive in remote regions of the Caucasus. There is no concrete evidence of this. But it may be noted that it was only in the British Isles and in northern and eastern France that harps were fairly frequently and clearly depicted between the eighth and twelfth centuries, and these are the very areas where there had been earlier 'culture-collisions' between indigenous, partly Christianized societies and those of invading Danes, Saxons and Franks.

Another possibility arises from the close links between the Celtic Christian communities of the British Isles and the Christian near East, Syria and Egypt in particular. Artists' transformation of foreign subjects and decorative motifs is too well documented to need elaboration here, but a musical parallel may be suggested in the adaptation of a foreign instrument. The vertical harps of the near East were well suited to their geographical situation. In a dry climate, a harp with a soundbox of thin wood covered with a skin belly, and gut strings twisted round a thin arm must have been light and easy to carry, even with the box upwards, and physically stable. If the same instrument were transported to a cold damp climate it would become much less stable and efficient. A similar instrument made more robustly, with a soundbox completely of wood, would have a different physical balance. If it also had strings fixed by the method used on Germanic lyres and on the Sutton Hoo harp and on all later harps, that is, fastened to a pin which passes through a solid frame or neck and is tuned by turning the pin, it would have needed a solid string-carrier, certainly much solider than the slender pole of the near-eastern harps. It would also have been extremely difficult to hold, let alone play, in the near-Eastern box-upwards position, and structurally impossible the other way up without some strain-carrying member (i.e. a forepillar) between string-carrier and box. In other words, Celtic harps might have originated as insular transformations of a near-Eastern instrument, incorporating certain structural features of robust native lyres, the whole adapted to the climate of north-western Europe.

It is extremely difficult to get a clear picture of musical practice in pre-Christian and early Christian Ireland. Few manuscripts are contemporary with or reasonably close in date and tradition to the events and situations with which they deal. While medieval re-workings of old Irish tales and myths and history tell us something about the attitude of medieval Irish people to their own inheritance, they tell us little that is specific about ancient Irish music. One of the few nearly contemporary references occurs in St. Adamnan's *Life of St. Columcille,* written early in the eighth century. Cronan, the pagan 'bard' with whom Columcille and his disciples conversed on the shores of Loch Cé, carried his instrument with him, but the disciples were disappointed that the saint did not ask Cronan to sing for them to the accompaniment of his *cruit.* The formal classification of music according to its function, of which the Irish *goltraige* (music of lamentation), *gentraige* (joyful music) and *súantraige* (sleep music) are examples, is of great antiquity and occurs in many civilizations. It even operates to a minute extent in present-day society, where, for example, no one would think of playing a funeral march at a wedding, or vice versa. Greek writers expended many words on the character and effect of different musical 'modes'. Put briefly and over-simply, in any musical system in which there are a number of 'scales' which have patterns of note-relationships that are different in each, there is a built-in, more or less ready-made musical character in each mode; one may sound more vigorous, another more languorous. On a small instrument of only five or six strings, such as a lyre, the player must retune to different modes for different kinds of music. If his lyre strings are fixed at the top to pins and are tuned by turning them, then a tuning key is needed. This is perhaps what is meant by *crann-gleasa,* literally tune-wood, for which the eighth-century brehon laws prescribed a sharp penalty if it were borrowed and not returned. According to these laws, players of the *cruit,* though not of the great status of poets, were freemen along with other skilled craftsmen such as smiths and physicians.

Of the many native and foreign elements which went to the

making of pre-Norman Irish society, the musical elements were part of oral craft traditions of which we have no record. But from the eleventh century onwards there is more concrete evidence about Irish music, harps and harpers. It comes partly from Irish sources and partly, as does much of our knowledge of later Irish music, from foreign observers. There is, of course, the old and now discredited tradition that the Irish harp now in Trinity College, Dublin, belonged to Brian Bóroime who became, in 1001, in effect the first high-king of all Ireland. Although that attribution for that harp cannot be justified, the implication that by the eleventh century the normal stringed instrument in Ireland was a harp and not a lyre seems to be correct.

The second Bishop of Dublin, chosen by the clergy and people of the then Norse-Irish city and consecrated by Archbishop Lanfranc in London in 1074, seems to have been a native Irishman trained at the Benedictine Abbey at Worcester under St. Wulfstan. In a long allegorical Latin poem,[1] Bishop Patrick made two interesting references to music and the *cithara*. The first is when one of three beautiful sisters, perhaps three of the Muses, teaches him songs.

> *Femina tum docuit (prima est) modulaminis odas*
> *Me cithara chordis que sex resonare solebat:*
> *Qua populis modulor, michimet que sepius utor.*

Then the woman (she was the first) taught me poems with
    well-contrived music
On a harp that sounded with six strings;
On it I make music for the people; more often I play it
    just for myself.'

Later in the same poem comes a description of a great city, its throngs and assemblies, feasts and music.

> *Quisque lyras aut omne genus modulaminis aptum*
> *Psalterium cytarasque novas aut organa terna?*

Who [can sing of] the lyres and every appropriate kind of
    well-contrived music
Psaltery, new harps and three-rank organ?

Bishop Patrick must have known the great organ at Winchester in England, but what was his 'new harp'? Was the six-stringed

[1] GWYNN, AUBREY: *The Writings of Bishop Patrick,* Dublin 1955.

cithara a lyre and the *cithara nova* a frame harp? It is perhaps more likely that the six-stringer was a small harp and the 'new harp' was bigger and had more strings. Certainly, the harp which is on the plaque attached to the Shrine of St. Mogue is a sizeable instrument (Plate 9). The plaque is generally thought to be of the eleventh century, though the shrine itself is older. It shows a seated, robed figure playing a harp above which is the bird who appears on some of the lyres on the Irish high crosses and with many David figures in English medieval illuminated manuscripts. The harp has a curved forepillar with a clearly-defined thickening which seems to be a T-formation, a shallow box, a gently curved neck in which there are ten or eleven pins, and eight or nine strings not properly aligned with the pins. The harp is on the player's left shoulder and he plucks the larger strings with the thumb and middle finger of his right hand. If this plaque is genuinely an eleventh-century piece, it appears that by this time there was already a harp with distinctly Irish characteristics. Eleventh-century English depictions of harps show an instrument with a slender forepillar which recalls that of the old quadrangular harp. In the twelfth century, English and

PLATE 9. *Figure with harp. Plaque on the Shrine of St. Mogue; 11th century*

continental sources show some harps with zoomorphic neck finials which slightly overhang the forepillars, and others in which the neck-to-forepillar joint has an upward sweep. The characteristic Irish T-formation of the forepillar is not shown on European harps, but a few illustrations of the twelfth and thirteenth centuries do show instruments which seem otherwise very close in structure to the known Irish harp. An excellent example is in a book of Latin psalms, canticles and prayers made some time before 1144 for Melissenda, daughter of Baldwin II, King of Jerusalem, and wife of Foulques, Count of Anjou (Plate 10). A throned David sits in the *Beatus* initial tuning a harp which has a thick curved forepillar and a solid overhanging neck. The whole book is an artistic amalgam; it is prefaced by a number of miniatures of the lives of Christ and the Virgin painted by a Greek artist, while among the scenes carved on its ivory cover is a David with his four attendant musicians, Ethan, Asaph, Eman and Idithun. David himself plays a *santir* (a near-Eastern dulcimer), and of the other figures, one tunes a quadrangular harp like that on the Castledermot cross while the others play a viol, a fiddle and a small, perfect, triangular harp with deep soundbox and curved forepillar.

PLATE 10. *David as harpist. Latin Psalter; 12th century*

4. The Medieval Irish harp

IN 1183, Giraldus de Barri, the Welsh-born Norman ecclesiastic whose family was heavily involved in the conquest of Ireland, paid his first visit to that country. He returned in 1185 with the English Prince John to whom he had by then become tutor. His enthusiastic comments on music and harp-playing in Ireland, written in Latin which is difficult both to translate and to interpret, have often been quoted, but no completely satisfactory elucidation has yet been arrived at. If, however, Giraldus's text is studied in conjunction with what is known of twelfth-century musical practice and with what is known quite precisely and unequivocally although from later sources about the nature of the Irish harp as a sound-maker, it becomes somewhat less enigmatic.

Giraldus went to Paris in 1167 and stayed there until 1172, studying the Latin poets, law, philosophy and theology. As a cleric, he must have been familiar with plainsong and, at least to some extent, with the practice of polyphony as it was used in the Church's liturgy. He must also have been familiar with the secular music which was played and sung in the households of feudal lords and in the capital cities of London and Paris. His literary and artistic standards were those of a cultivated western European ecclesiastic, not of an out-back Norman-Welshman.

In his *Topographica Hiberniae*,[2] Giraldus berated the Irish as 'barbarians' for what he considered to be their lack of industry, their poor husbandry and disinterest in city life, their flowing beards and odd clothes, their love of leisure and liberty. He granted them splendour of physique and superlative skill in the practice of instrumental music. Whatever music Giraldus heard in Ireland, it did not sound to him barbarous and peculiar; he described it specifically as better executed and more agreeable than that generally heard in England. Whatever its musical idiom was, it seems to have been not far removed from that of Western Christendom, and if we examine Giraldus's words, it appears that he tried to be as explicit as possible in Latin, a language whose

[2]GIRALDUS CAMBRENSIS: *Topographiae*, Rolls Series, Vol. V.

vocabulary was not geared to the expression of musical subtleties.
His section on Irish instrumental music is worth quoting in full:

I find among these people commendable diligence only on
musical instruments, on which they are incomparably more
skilled than any nation I have seen. Their style is not, as on the
British instruments to which we are accustomed, deliberate and
solemn but quick and lively; nevertheless the sound is smooth
and pleasant.

It is remarkable that, with such rapid fingerwork, the musical
rhythm is maintained and that, by unfailingly disciplined art,
the integrity of the tune is fully preserved throughout the ornate
rhythms and the profusely intricate polyphony—and with such
smooth rapidity, such 'unequal equality', such 'discordant
concord'. Whether the strings strike together a fourth or a fifth,
[the players] nevertheless always start from B flat and return to
the same, so that everything is rounded off in a pleasant general
sonority. They introduce and leave rhythmic motifs so subtly,
they play the tinkling sounds on the thinner strings above the
sustained sound of the thicker string so freely, they take such
secret delight and caress [the strings] so sensuously, that the
greatest part of their art seems to lie in veiling it, as if 'That which
is concealed is bettered—art revealed is art shamed'.

Thus it happens that those things which bring private and
ineffable delight to people of subtle appreciation and sharp
discernment, burden rather than delight the ears of those who,
in spite of looking do not see and in spite of hearing do not
understand; to unwilling listeners, fastidious things appear
tedious and have a confused and disordered sound.

One must note that both Scotland and Wales, the latter by
virtue of extension, the former by affinity and intercourse,
depend on teaching to imitate and rival Ireland in musical
practice. Ireland uses and delights in two instruments only,
the *cithara* and the *tympanum*. Scotland uses three, the *cithara*,
the *tympanum* and the *chorus*. Wales uses the *cithara*, *tibiae* and
chorus. Also, they use strings made of brass not of leather.
However, in the opinion of many, Scotland today not only
equals Ireland, her mistress, but also by far outdoes and surpasses
her in musical skill. Hence many people already look there as
though to the source of the art.

Cithara was a harp. *Tympanum* possibly meant a bowed or beaten lyre, perhaps adopted from the Norsemen, for some forms of these still survive in Scandinavia. *Tibiae* were pipes, though Giraldus did not specify what kind. The description of musical performance obviously refers to harp-playing; on a lyre, whether plucked or bowed, there is no possibility of such intricacy. The Latin terms which Giraldus used cannot be put exactly into modern musical terminology for our conception and practice of music are greatly different from those of medieval people. His key words, however, are all to do with particular aspects and styles of polyphonic music as distinct from monophonic music such as plainsong and presumably much secular vocal music of that time.

While the first paragraph describes the general agreeableness of Irish performance, the second seems to describe the playing of florid elaborations in impeccable rhythm, proportion and clarity. And we may note here that it was precisely these qualities that Edward Bunting praised, six hundred years later, in Denis Hempson, last of the harpers in the traditional style. The word translated here as 'polyphony' is *organa*. In the twelfth century, *organa* meant, in one sense, the organ, as in the already-quoted eleventh century poem by Bishop Patrick. It was also the plural of *organum*, which denoted both a particular polyphonic technique—that of adding one florid part above a slow-moving *tenor*—and a piece composed in that technique. Explanatory translations of Giraldus's *organa* would be 'varieties of music in parts' or 'pieces of part music'. What is here translated as *ornate rhythms* is in the original *crispatos modulos*. The latter means literally 'measurement', *cantus crispus* is known early in the sixteenth century in England as a term for very florid polyphony in many parts, and its musical use is a metaphor taken from the primary meaning of *crispus*, which is curly or quivering. Irish harpers were, according to this account, incomparably skilled in contriving and playing two-part music with a complex and brilliant upper part, and Giraldus, having first described it in technical terms, reinforces this with a physical description—the tinkling of the high strings over the heavier sound of the bass strings.

The curious second sentence in the second paragraph has puzzled many scholars. The 'fourths and fifths' are exactly those intervals which generally occur at structural points between *tenor* and added upper part in written polyphony dating from the twelfth century.

The 'starting and ending with B flat', however, is enigmatic. But since Giraldus had already dealt with the rhythmic structure and technical execution of the music played by the Irish harpers, it is not unlikely that what he referred to here was its melodic idiom— an aspect of music notoriously difficult to describe. Technical elaboration of this point is not possible in a short monograph, but what Giraldus may have been trying to say is that the actual tune material used by the Irish harpers began and ended with a flat seventh-note-of-the-scale in close proximity to the tonic note. Though we have no written record of Irish tunes from so early a date, the melodic formulae of some old Irish tunes which were first written down in the eighteenth century suggests that this may indeed have been the case.

The end of the second paragraph contains what is surely a perfect description of a virtuoso savouring his own virtuosity, and the third, a perfect snobbish comment on uninformed audiences, which was echoed in similar terms a century later by Johannes de Grocheo writing about the then new musical form, the motet.

The Irish harpers of the twelfth century were, like other medieval instrumentalists, craft musicians whose repertoires and skills were transmitted entirely orally, and they must have been professionals of the highest order. It is likely that all kinds of music flourished, along with literary and other artistic activity, in that century of comparative quiet after the long years of Viking power; though we have only one example from Ireland of learned, written-down vocal polyphony—a tiny three-part morsel in *discantus* style[3]—it is pre-Norman and certainly the work of an Irishman. It is at least contemporary with and perhaps ante-dates the earliest examples of three-part music which come from the cathedral of Notre Dame in Paris. Some of the complex syllabic verse of the medieval *fili*, who were heirs to much of the tradition of the philosopher-seers of pre-Christian Ireland, was written down for their patrons. But the arts of the reciters and of the harpers who, like the *cruit*-players of earlier times, joined with them in the performance of the poets' songs, eulogies and satires, have passed away without record.

Whatever those arts were, they must have been as attractive to the conquering Norman invaders as many other aspects of Gaelic-

---

[3] HARRISON, F. LL.: *Polyphony In Medieval Ireland* in *Festschrift Bruno Stäblein*, Erlangan, 1967.

PLATE II. *Trinity College harp. 14th century*

Irish society, and the 'Gaelicisation' in varying degrees of Norman and English settlers during the thirteenth and fourteenth centuries is surely a tribute to the vigour and calibre of Gaelic-Irish artistic life. It was during the thirteenth century that the standard bardic language which was to be used in Ireland and Scotland for the next three hundred years emerged, and it is possible that the harping style which was associated with the performance of sung or chanted works in that language evolved during the same period. While we shall never know exactly what the style was, we can have some idea of the sound of the medieval Irish harpers' instrument, for the earliest surviving specimen of an Irish harp—the famous instrument which dates probably from the fourteenth century and is now preserved in Trinity College, Dublin—was playable to some extent during the process of restoration in 1961.

This little harp (Plate 11) is about seventy centimetres high and had originally thirty strings, of which twenty-nine are strung at present. When diatonically tuned, this gives a range of four octaves, which is the largest of any type of medieval instrument other than the organ. Since pre-sixteenth-century brass was closer to bronze than to the modern metal of the same name, present-day brass strings cannot sound exactly like the original strings. But the sound of the Trinity College harp when played with long finger-nails in the old Irish way is extraordinarily sweet and clear, with a quality which is somewhat bell-like but with an added richness akin to that of a guitar. Giraldus's word for the sound of the upper strings, *tinitus* or tinkling, seems to have been particularly apt, and it suggests that the Irish harps had already in the twelfth century a tonal character similar to the harps of the fourteenth and fifteenth centuries. We know little about medieval harp techniques elsewhere in Europe. Strings of metal, though not necessarily of brass were used on some harps, and there are several references to playing with nails like 'Teach him to harpe with his nayles scharpe' which occurs in the thirteenth-century 'Kyng Horn'. But since no European instrument is known to have had the rugged structure of the Irish harp and certainly none had the great one-piece willow soundbox, a considerably different technique must have been needed for them. The use of thumb and first two fingers only, rather than the thumb-and-three-fingers of later harp techniques is suggested by much European iconographical evidence and verified by well-document-ed conservative practice in the seventeenth century. It may or may

PLATE 12. *Queen Mary harp. 15th century*

not have been used on medieval Irish harps—long nails do, in fact, give a great degree of mobility over the whole hand, provided it is not held in the position of modern harp-playing. But we really know as little of medieval Irish harpers' techniques as of their repertoire. What did they play as a background to the declaiming or chanting of poetry, of panegyrics and satires, or as banquet music for the powerful nobility, Anglo-Irish as well as Gaelic, who maintained and hired them? We shall never know. What is certain is that in musical matters, medieval re-workings of old Irish material frequently incorporate conceptions and practices more typical of the time of the medieval written forms than of the time of the original events. For example, the opening of the Glenmason version of the Story of Deirdre and the Children of Uisneach, which probably dates from the fifteenth century, describes a feast given by Conor and the nobles of Ulster at which many musicians and poets stood up to perform 'songs and lays and chants and to recite genealogies and branches of relationship'. The ninth century version of the story has no such scene. This is not to say that eulogistic and epic performances had not taken place at lordly feasts in pre-Christian Ireland, but to emphasise that the picture here is on a medieval, not an ancient Celtic scale. For the scribe of the Glenmason version of that tale, the living musical association of the kind of scene he described must have been the sound of a harp like the Trinity College harp.

The two other extant examples of the small low-headed Irish harp are known as the Lamont harp and the Queen Mary harp (Plates 12 and 13). Both come from Scotland, where a Gaelic civilization which had much in common with that of Ireland flourished in the Highlands and Western Isles. They are thus Irish by organological classification, not by provenance. Their structure is identical with that of the Trinity College harp, their proportions vary slightly but not significantly from it. They are made entirely of hornbeam, a tree not native to Scotland.

There seems to be only one contemporary depiction of the small Irish harp—that on the stone tomb at Jerpoint Abbey in County Kilkenny on which is carved a figure of recumbent warrior with a harp at his side (Plate 14). The stone is now worn, but the structure of the harp, the carved T-formation on the forepillar and the 'cheek-bands' on the neck can still be seen. A gravestone at Kiells, in Argyllshire, Scotland, which dates from about 1500, shows a

PLATE 13. *Lamont harp. 15th century*

curious hybrid with forepillar and neck like one form of Renaissance harp and a huge soundbox covered with Celtic-style decorations.

Although in Ireland and Wales in later centuries the harp became associated to a great extent with what is loosely called 'folk-music', this was the result of particular political and social circumstances. The harp has generally been an aristocratic, high art instrument, and nowhere more so than in Ireland in medieval times. It was a valuable object, produced by an expert instrument maker and often exquisitely decorated. A harper was a skilled specialist musician, and no poor man could have maintained or hired one, any more than he could maintain a racehorse today. The patrons of men of learning, of poets, reciters and harpers, were the Gaelic Irish aristocracy, the Norman-Irish who eventually became indistinguishable in English government eyes from the native lords and, later, the powerful Anglo-Irish families like the Butlers who were Earls of Ormond, and the Fitzgeralds—descendants of Giraldus de Barri's Welsh-Norman uncle, Maurice, who were Earls of Desmond and Kildare. Two of the most beautiful Irish harps which survive from the beginning of the seventeenth century have associations with the Fitzgeralds (Plates 20 and 23).

English kings, from Henry II in the twelfth century to Edward IV in the middle of the fifteenth involved themselves in varying degrees in the political 'problem of Ireland'. Nevertheless, whatever the swings and balances of power between Gael and Anglo-Irish

PLATE 14. *Stone figure of recumbent knight with small harp. Jerpoint Abbey; 15th century*

were, society in Ireland outside a few towns and the small, purely English settlement around Dublin known as The Pale, was essentially Irish, both in language and culture. From the time of Henry VII, however, the English government became directly and more aggressively involved in Ireland, partly as a result of the Yorkist sympathies of some of the Anglo-Irish lords, and later, under Henry VIII and Elizabeth I, for religious as well as political reasons. During the succeeding centuries of Anglicization, from the comparatively peaceful submissions of forty Gaelic and Anglo-Irish lords to Henry VIII by 1547 to the brutal violence of Cromwell and the forcible 'protestantization' following the Battle of the Boyne and the Treaty of Limerick, Irish society was first disrupted and then destroyed. Our knowledge of the art of Irish harpers and of their instruments during the sixteenth and seventeenth centuries comes, ironically, largely from English sources.

5. The Large Irish Harp

To the English government officials of sixteenth-century Ireland, 'harpers, rhymers, Irish chroniclers, bards, etc.' were seditious and dangerous persons. Their poetry and music, however, were agreeable even to 'gentlemen in the English Pale' and their presence there under any pretext whatever was ultimately forbidden. Observers from less politically conscious spheres gave more precise accounts of the activity of Irish poets and harpers. The English Jesuit, William Good, who taught in Ireland in the middle of the sixteenth century wrote of the Irish people: 'They love music mightily and of all instruments are particularly taken with the harp, which being strung with brass wire and beaten with crooked nails, is very melodious'. The English poet, Edmund Spenser not unnaturally noticed the work of Irish practitioners in his own trade. He wrote:

> I have caused divers of [their poems] to be translated unto me and surely they savoured of sweete wit and good invention, but skilled not of the goodly ornaments of poetry; yet were they sprinkled with some pretty flowers of their own natural device, which gave good grace and comeliness unto them . . .

> Theyr [the poets'] verses are usually songe at all feasts and meetings, by certayne other persons, whose proper function that is . . .

There is a more detailed account in the Clanricarde Memoirs.

> The Action and Pronunciation of the Poem in the Presence . . . of the principal Person it related to, was performed with a great deal of Ceremony, in a Consort of Vocal and Instrumental Musick. The Poet himself said nothing, but directed and took care, that everybody else did his part right. The Bards having first had the Composition from him, got it well by heart, and now pronounced it orderly, keeping even pace with a Harp, touch'd upon that Occasion; no other musical Instrument being allow'd of for the said Purpose than this alone.

The same kind of partnership of words and music exists, though in a very different idiom, between a virtuoso calypso singer and his guitarist. And this, too, is a form in which, but for the grace of sound recording, the unwritten music would be as lost to future generations as is that of the Irish harpers.

Thomas Smith, an English agent, gave a pompously disapproving account of the chanting of a praise poem to a chieftain who had just completed a successful cattle raid, or *creach*.

> Now comes the rimer that made the rime, with his rakry. The rakry is he that shall utter the rime and the rimer himself sits by with the captain very proudly. He brings with him also his harper who plays all the while that the rakry sings the rime. Also he hath his bard, which is a kind of foolish fellow, who must also have a horse given him. The harper must have a new saffron shirt and a mantle and a hackney; and the rakry must have twenty or thirty kine and the rimer himself horse and harness, with a nag to ride on, a silver goblet, a pair of beads of coral,

PLATE 15. *Reciter and harper performing before a chief. John Derricke,* Image of Ireland, *1581*

with buttons of silver—and this, with more, they look you to have, for destruction of the commonwealth and to the blasphemy of God; and this is the best thing that the rimers cause them to do.

There is in Derricke's *Image of Ireland*, of 1578—a very anti-Irish image, it must be said—a picture of the kind of scene Smyth described (Plate 15). The lord sits at table while food is prepared nearby, over an open fire. The *recaire* (Smyth's rakry) holds forth, arms dramatically outstretched, while the harper sits on the ground behind him, playing. The instrument, however, is nothing more than a formalised and inaccurate depiction of a non-Irish harp, its strings running absurdly from soundbox to forepillar.

On the continent, the Irish harp must have been known simply as a musical instrument, not in the specifically Irish rôle which so infuriated English officialdom. We know little about the extent to which Irish harpers moved outside Ireland and Scotland in medieval times. In the twelfth century, John of Salisbury, describing one of the Crusades of the previous century, wrote that there would have been no music at all if it had not been for the Irish harp, and some players must surely have travelled the great (and profitable) pilgrim routes. The skill of the Irish harpers was certainly famous in Europe in the latter part of the sixteenth century when Vincenzo Galilei described them in *Dialogo della Musica Antica e della Moderna*[4] which was published in Florence in 1581. Galilei was one of a number of high-born Italian amateurs of that time who wrote at length, and in bitter disagreement with each other, about musical theory and practice, both ancient and modern. His writings contain a good deal of nonsense about the music of antiquity, but he does appear to have examined an Irish harp and his comments are not only interesting in themselves but significant when related to other material.

Among the stringed instruments now played in Italy there is first of all the Harp, which is none other than the ancient Cithara with many strings. The form indeed is different in each case, but only because of the different workmanship of those days, and from the greater number of strings and their thickness. It

[4]GALILEI, VINCENZO: *Dialogo Della Musica Antica Et Moderna,* Florence, 1581.

contains from the lowest note to the highest note more than three octaves.

This most ancient instrument was brought to us (as Dante commented) from Ireland, where it is excellently made and in great quantities. The people of that island play it a great deal and have done so for many centuries, also it is the special emblem of the realm, where it is depicted and sculptured on public buildings and on coins. From which, it may be deduced to be descended from the Prophet, King David. The harps in use among that people are somewhat bigger than ordinary ones. They have generally strings of brass, with a few of steel in the top register, like the Harpsichord. The players keep the fingernails of both hands rather long, shaping them carefully like the quills of the jacks which strike the strings of the Spinet. The number of these is fifty-four, fifty-six or even sixty. Nevertheless, among the Hebrews, we learn that the Cithara, or Psaltery of the Prophet had the number of ten.

A few months ago (through the offices of a most courteous Irish gentleman) I carefully examined the stringing of that kind

PLATE 16. *Irish groat of Henry VIII*

of harp. I find it to be the same as that which, with double the number of strings, was introduced into Italy a few years ago, although some (against all good reasoning) say that they themselves have newly invented it, trying to persuade the uninformed that they alone know how to play it and understand how to tune it.

Parts of what Galilei wrote are verifiable from other sources. If frequency of depiction is anything to go by, harps seem to have been rare in Italy in the twelfth and thirteenth centuries. While *Beatus* and *Exultate* initials in English and French illuminated psalters of that time abound with harp-playing Davids, those in Italian manuscripts do not; and if the frame-harp was a northwest-European instrument originally, it must have been introduced into Italy from somewhere, and Ireland is as likely a source as any other. The range of 'more than three octaves' for the harp ordinarily in use in Italy in the second half of the sixteenth century agrees exactly with that of Italian and South German harps which survive from that period. Galilei was certainly correct in his observations about the popularity of the harp in Ireland and its use on coinage (Plate 16), though we do not know, in the absence of any extant examples, whether it was sculptured on public buildings.

No complete late sixteenth-century Irish harp is known to exist, but the Ballinderry fragments (Plates 17 and 18) are almost certainly of this date. They consist of the 'cheek-bands' from the neck, a number of tuning pins, the decorative boss from the neck finial and the neck-to-forepillar brace of a very large, low-headed Irish harp which would certainly have been bigger than the normal Renaissance harp. The 'fifty-four, fifty-six or even sixty' strings seems to mean those of the Harpsichord or Spinet, the last figure giving the five chromatic octaves of a big instrument. (Galilei's characteristically illogical sequence of statements is apparent even in this short extract). If he did mean it to refer to a harp, then it must apply, not to the Irish harp but to 'that which, with double the number of strings [of the Irish harp] was introduced into Italy a few years ago'. The instrument Galilei was writing about in this last paragraph was the big chromatic harp with two ranks of strings, which was introduced into Italy, probably from Flanders, in the middle of the century. Later in the *Dialogo* he gave a stringing plan for one of these, with fifty-eight strings.

There is no real resemblance, apart from the general one of overall size, between a big Irish harp and these chromatic harps. Galilei was probably using the fact that he had seen an Irish harp as a piece of 'insidemanship' against the views and claims of other factions among Italian musicians, those of Zarlino in particular, of which he disapproved. He may also have confused claims about the big two-rank chromatic harp, which was probably not invented in Italy, with those regarding the three-rank harp, later known as the triple harp, which was.

Galilei did not say who his 'most courteous Irish gentleman' was and we can speculate on his identity and what took him to Florence. Was he the harper of an Irish lord, attending him abroad, or an Irish gentleman who played it himself? There is very little concrete evidence as to when Irish gentlemen-amateurs began to play the harp in Ireland. Another unanswered question is the origin and significance of the word *clarsach*, literally 'little flat thing'. It was

PLATE 17. *Ballinderry fragments. 16th century*

used of some harps from the late fifteenth century in Scotland and in Ireland from the sixteenth century onwards, in addition to the older word *cruit*.

Very few Irish harps carry makers' names. The anonymous craftsmen of the late sixteenth and early seventeenth centuries must however have been as musically aware and acoustically conscious as good instrument builders elsewhere. The differences between the soundboxes of the smaller, earlier instruments and

PLATE 18. *Detail of 17*

those of the large seventeenth century Irish harps was described in the first chapter. It is possible that when the Irish harp was made considerably bigger—perhaps for use as a bass instrument like other new harps of the early baroque period—there was some inadequacy of sonority in the middle and upper registers and it was no longer so effective as a solo instrument. Whatever the reason, the soundboxes of all Irish harps made from the early seventeenth century onwards have the subtle increase in depth as they get narrower towards the treble end, so that the resonance chamber under the shorter strings is bigger in relation to them than it was in the earlier harps.

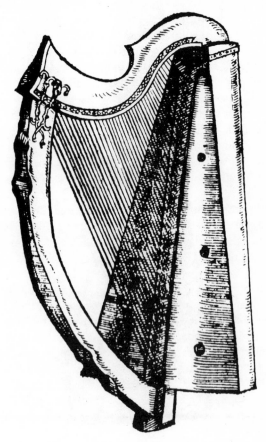

PLATE 19. *Irish Harp. Michael Praetorius,* Syntagma Musicum, *1619*

The sonority of the Irish harp, produced by plucking with what were, in effect, horn plectra on thick brass strings attached to a huge resonator, was peculiarly related to the musical idiom and environment in which it evolved. Francis Bacon wrote in *Sylva Sylvarum* 'No harp hath the sound so melting and prolonged as the Irish harp' and in this effect of prolongation of very sweet sound, both the unique charm and the eventual decline and disappearance of the instrument surely lie. Put in oversimple terms, with music made in the old fixed modes there are hardly any note contradictions possible within a single piece. The system of major and minor keys with identical note relationships and a large number of chromatic possibilities evolved fully during the seventeenth century; with music in this system, tunes may change key and in order to do so must use note modifications (chromatic notes), besides inevitably implying beneath themselves a substructure of moving harmony, which modal tunes do not necessarily do. An instrument with long resonance is ideally suited to music in the one system, less so to music in the other, and totally unsuited to music which goes beyond a certain point of chromatic complexity, even if the strings can be tuned to cope with it literally. (In this connection it must be remembered that the great growth of music for keyboard instruments, with their sound-stopping mechanisms, coincided with the high development of the major-minor system.)

It is possible that when the Earls of Tyrone and Tyrconnell and nearly one hundred of the leading Irishmen of Ulster left their native land in 1607 and went into exile on the continent rather than live in an Ireland which was increasingly under English domination, they took harpers with them. The instrument was familiar, in some European circles at least, as an 'exotic' kind of harp. For example, the 1638 inventory of the Hofkapelle of the Landgraf of Hesse at Kassel included 'an old Irish harp', and the earnest Lutheran choirmaster-pedagogue, Michael Praetorius, gave a short description and an illustration of an Irish harp in his *Syntagma Musicum* of 1619 (Plate 19). The harp section of his book is not wholly reliable.[5] The 'ordinary harp' is correct in terms of contemporary German usage but the 'great double harp' is a misconception and Praetorius cannot have known that instrument at first

---

[5] PRAETORIUS, MICHAEL: *Syntagma Musicum*, Vol. 2. Wolfenbüttel, 1619.

hand. His illustration of an Irish harp shows an instrument very like that which is implied by the Ballinderry fragments, and it has a box which deepens towards the narrow end. It is however, strung on the right side of the neck. This misconception may have been the result of an assumption that, because the instrument was held on the left shoulder, not the right as with most European harps, it was also strung in reverse. It may only have been poor observation on the part of the artist. Praetorius's text on the Irish harp reads:

> Irish harp, *Harpa Irlandica,* apparently has great thick brass strings, to the number of forty-three, and one of the most beautiful sonorities.

He then went on to give a partly-chromatic tuning for these forty-three strings which not only contains obvious printing errors but is technically and practically absurd. It does, however, contain elements of musical sense, and it seems possible that there were some Irish harps at about this time which were partly chromatically tuned. A modally or diatonically tuned harp with as many as forty-three strings would have a range of six octaves, unusual at that time even on keyboard instruments.

It was stated in an 'Ancient History of Kerry',[6] written in the

[6]PRENDERGAST, JARLATH, (ed.): *The O'Gorman Manuscript in Cork Historical Archaeological Journal,* Vol. 6, 1898–9.

PLATE 20. *Dalway fragments. 1621*

middle of the eighteenth century, that Nicholas Dall Pierse, a blind Kerry harper of high reputation who lived from 1561 to 1653 'completed the harp with more wires'. We cannot now tell whether in fact he did, or whether it was merely a general trend at that time. An ode to Pierse written about 1600 contains a reference to the 'vigour of eight fingers' which may perhaps be taken as evidence that Irish harpers by this time used a thumb-and-three-finger technique even if they had used thumb and two fingers in medieval times. Again, it may be no more than poetic lack of observation of the fact that harpers use thumbs but never little fingers.

Only one early seventeenth-century Irish harp has as great a number of strings as Praetorius gave, and it is something of an enigma in other ways. The Dalway fragments (Plate 20) consist of the complete neck and nearly complete forepillar of a harp made in 1621 for one of the Fitzgerald family. There are forty-five pin-holes along the neck and seven additional ones in the middle which must have carried strings parallel to the primary rank. These were probably sympathetic, not struck strings, added at a point where the sonority of the harp was weak. Perhaps the now-lost box was of the older kind, of the same depth all through. Of the other large low-headed harps, the Otway and the O ffogerty harps (Plates 21 and 22) both have thirty-five strings and the beautiful Fitzgerald-Kildare harp (Plates 23 and 24), which in some ways foreshadows the high-headed form, had originally thirty-nine.

The large low-headed Irish harp was played to some extent in England in the seventeenth century. The *Ayres and Dialogues* and *Mottects or Grave Chamber Musique* of Martin Peerson, issued in London in 1620 and 1630 respectively, seem to be the only published works which mention it by name. It is given on the title page of the *Mottects* along with virginals, bass-lute and bandora as an alternative 'for want of organs'—not, one suspects, a highly practical alternative—and it is mentioned in the composer's foreword to the *Ayres and Dialogues*. John Evelyn wrote in his Diary in 1654:

In my judgement it is far superior to the lute itself, or whatever speaks with strings.

And in 1668:

. . . my worthy friend Mr. Clarke, who makes it execute lute, viol, and all the harmony an instrument is capable of. Pity it is that it is not more in use; but indeed, to play well takes up the whole man, as Mr. Clarke has assured me, who, though a gentleman of quality and parts, was yet brought up to that instrument from five years old.

PLATE 21. *Otway harp. 17th century*

PLATE 22. *O ffogerty harp. 17th century*

PLATE 23. *Fitzgerald-Kildare harp. Early 17th century*

The English gentleman who played the Irish harp was almost certainly not using the traditional long-fingernail technique. The observant Evelyn would surely have commented on such a curious and 'ungentlemanly' phenomenon. There is no mention of it either in the writings of James Talbot, Regius Professor of Hebrew at Cambridge from 1689 to 1704,[7] who measured and made copious notes on most of the musical instruments which were in use in England in the last part of the seventeenth century. His descriptions of the large low-headed Irish harp (Plate 25) were remarkably accurate and provide a number of interesting details, like the fact that Irish harps were made in England, where the soundboxes were, of course, of the traditional and indispensable willow, but the necks and forepillars were made of walnut. Like Praetorius, he gave the number of strings as forty-three though

[7]RIMMER, JOAN: *James Talbot's Manuscript VI—Harps* in *Galpin Society Journal* xvi, 1963; and *The Morphology of the Irish Harp* in *Galpin Society Journal* xvii, 1964.

PLATE 24. *Detail of 23*

sometimes forty. He also described a way of tuning the harp in upper and lower sections separately, with a duplicated note, or 'wolf', at the point of division, which accords with later Irish sources. He did not say explicitly whether the tuning of a forty-three string Irish harp was diatonic or chromatic; but he did say that a thirty-six string harp 'includes five octaves', which means that it was not chromatic.

An interesting comment on this occurs in the *Memoirs* of Arthur

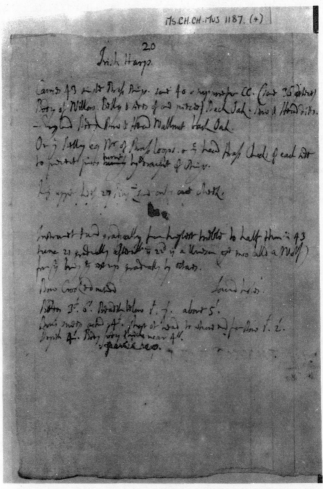

PLATE 25. *Notes on the Irish Harp by James Talbot. c 1690*

O'Neill,[8] an Irish harper who lived from 1737 to 1816. When in County Longford, he visited Connor Kelly, a local harp-maker, while he was making an instrument. When it was finished 'it had to be taken asunder, as when it was tuned the treble was thought too long. It had forty strings, thirty-five in general being considered enough. The harp was a second time put together and turned out the best one I ever heard or played upon.'

In Ireland in the seventeenth century the pattern of society was changing drastically. The old patrons of poetry and music were exiled or reduced in power and wealth. But as Brian Ó Cuiv has pointed out, the poorer Gaelic-speaking people had less to lose from the disruption of the older Irish society. They allied themselves to and intermarried with the English and Scottish settlers and formed the beginnings of a middle class, prosperous enough but lacking the cohesive traditions, grandeur and taste of pre-Cromwellian Ireland. We cannot be sure how much of the old truly Irish musical tradition survived the seventeenth century. Just as elaborate syllabic court poetry disappeared and simpler accentual verse was composed, so it seems likely that much of the intricate high art of the earlier Irish harpers was lost. We know more about the Irish harpers of the eighteenth century than about any earlier players and it is obvious that their instruments, technique and musical style were subject to many non-Irish influences. Their repertoire consisted mainly of tunes of Irish association, simply but movingly played on harps which retained enough of the tonal charm of the older Irish harp to have still a special character and quality. Judging from material published first in the eighteenth century, some of the tunes were probably very ancient, perhaps drawn from the old aristocratic repertory and from venerable though unrecorded popular usage. A few were of Scottish, English or Italian derivation. But it is probable that the style of some of what we now consider traditional Irish music evolved in the late seventeenth and early eighteenth centuries as a hybrid of largely unrecorded indigenous music and imported foreign styles. This phenomenon has been common enough in other art forms throughout Irish history.

Though the typical Irish harps of the eighteenth century

[8] O'NEILL, ARTHUR: 'Memoir', in Donal O'Sullivan, *Carolan*, London, 1958.

PLATE 26. *Sirr harp. 18th century*

(Plates 26, 27, 28 and 29) still had the big one-piece soundbox, their superstructure was different from that of the earlier instruments. They were larger overall and they were high-headed like some of the English and Welsh triple harps—that is, the forepillar, now only slightly curved, was very tall, the neck swept upwards to meet it and the bass strings were therefore much longer in relation to the treble strings than those of the low-headed harps. Surviving examples are roughly made, compared with the beautiful low-headed instruments and, apart from one rather curious harp (Plate 30) made for a gentleman amateur, they are not integrally decorated.

These were the harps of the itinerant harpers of the eighteenth century (Plates 31, 32), many of them blind like Turlough O'Carolan. They lived the hard life of a musical 'commercial traveller', going on horseback from one gentleman's house to another, playing Irish music and sometimes composing it too. Most of them played with the finger-tips, not with nails, and by 1792, when the famous Belfast Harp Meeting was held, only one of the ten players used the old method.

PLATE 27. *Back view of 26*

PLATE 28. *Mullagh Mast harp. 18th century*

PLATE 29. *O'Neill harp. 18th century*

PLATE 30. *Bunworth harp by John Kelly. 1734*

The final irony in the history of the Irish harp is that a general public interest, particularly among townspeople, in Irish music and the harp which had been associated with it began to arise at the very time when the instrument itself and the characteristic way of playing were fast disappearing. Patrick MacDonald, who published a collection of Highland Vocal Airs in 1790, wrote in his Preface:

> In Ireland, the harpers, the original composers and chief depositories of that music [i.e. Gaelic music], have, till lately, been uniformly cherished and supported by the nobility and gentry. They endeavoured to outdo one another in playing the airs that were most esteemed with correctness and with their proper expression. Such of them as were men of ability attempted to adorn them with graces and variations or to produce what were called good sets of them. These were communicated to their successors and by them transmitted with additions . . . and so long as they continued in the hands of the native harpers, we may suppose that they were gradually improved, as whatever graces and variations they added to them were consistent with a tendency to heighten and display the genuine spirit and expression of the music. The taste for that style of performance seems now, however, to be declining. The native harpers are not much encouraged.

In Ireland at the end of the eighteenth and the beginning of the nineteenth century there was indeed an awakening interest in Irish music, but it was for Irish music in an acceptable form of packaging. The public in Ireland disapproved quite rightly of Beethoven's bombastically inappropriate settings of Irish songs, but they also allowed the last remnants of their own great harping tradition to disappear. Their taste was for something in between. As MacDonald implied, the performing style of the old harpers was too remote from the musical fashions of post-Revolutionary Europe, which obtained in Ireland as much as anywhere.

If it were not for the careful work of Edward Bunting,[9] then a young assistant organist at St. Anne's Church in Belfast, in noting down the music of some of the last Irish harpers, we should have

---

[9]BUNTING, EDWARD: *Ancient Irish Music*, Dublin, 1796 and 1809 and *Ancient Music of Ireland*, Dublin, 1840.

PLATE 31. *Carolan harp. Late 17th or early 18th century*

no idea today of what that style was. There had been some attempts to maintain and encourage public interest in the old harpers, and to provide money for them by the now time-honoured method of holding festivals. Annual festivals, or 'balls' as Arthur O'Neill called them in his Memoir, were held at Granard from 1781 to 1785, with up to eleven performers, prize money of seven, five, three and two guineas, and in the last one, subscriptions for all the players regardless of whether they won prizes or not. Edward Bunting was engaged to note down the tunes played at the four-day-long Festival held in Belfast in 1792. He not only did this but also made notes on the style of performance in general, and these are of the greatest value, even though his memory seems to have become uncertain in some respects when he worked on his notes many years later. He wrote that he was

> very much surprised to find that all the Melodies played by the harpers were performed with so much quickness that they did not bear the least comparison with the manner in which he had been accustomed to hear them played on the flute, violin, etc.,

PLATE 32. *Back view of 31*

PLATE 33. *Downhill harp by Cormac O'Kelly. 1702*

by the Professors of those instruments, who usually performed them so slow that the melody was nearly lost, and they were sung by the better class of people in the same drawling sleepy style.

Bunting himself was often complimented on the way he played Irish airs on the piano, and he said that he claimed

no merit . . . than that of playing the melodies quicker and in humble imitation of that animated manner peculiar to the old harpers.

He was not an Irish speaker and the vocabulary of musical terms and formulae used by the harpers, which he took down more or less phonetically in English, had to be edited later by a competent Irish scholar. Denis Hempson, the one player who used the old finger-nail technique, was ninety-seven years of age at the time of this festival. Blinded in childhood, he was the only one whose repertory and style of performance in certain pieces were still close to medieval harping, and the importance of Bunting's notation of some of his performances cannot be overestimated. Hempson's harp was the beautiful instrument now known as the Downhill harp (Plates 33–34). It was made in 1702 by Cormac O'Kelly of Ballynascreen,

PLATE 34. *Detail of 33*

County Derry, but, like its owner, it was not typical of the eighteenth century for it is essentially a low-headed harp.

During the first two decades of the nineteenth century, most of the old harpers were dying in obscurity and probably penury, except for a few who ended their days as pensioners of kindly gentlemen. Two Harp Societies, one in Belfast and one in Dublin, were founded with the object of 'reviving the harp and the ancient music of Ireland', largely by teaching poor and blind children. Of this, George Petrie observed tartly that 'the effort . . . to perpetuate the existence of the harp in Ireland, by trying to give the harpers' skill to a number of poor blind boys, was at once a benevolent and a patriotic one: but it was a delusion'.

The 'harpers' skill' was, of course, the particular skill of the Irish kind of harper on the Irish kind of harp. Even if the efforts of the Harp Societies had been a lot more successful than they were, it is extremely unlikely that the traditional instrument itself could have been perpetuated, for making a true Irish harp was as special a skill as playing one, and city makers did not make them. The instrument's big, sweet sonority and non-chromatic tuning were out of place in the musical world of the early eighteen-hundreds. While the harpers of sixteenth-century Ireland had been able to turn their aristocratic skills to other kinds of music when the old Gaelic world was burst apart, the eighteenth-century harpers, already archaic and somewhat anachronistic, could not adapt to the nineteenth century. By the end of that century's second decade the old Irish harp was gone.

6. *The Neo-Irish Harp*

THE instruments which the Dublin harp-maker, John Egan, and his nephew and successor Francis Hewson made for the Harp Societies and other interested amateurs were of two kinds and neither was like the old Irish harp. They were much more lightly constructed; their soundboxes were made like those of the pedal harp, with thin bellies and separate, rounded backs; the strings were fixed in the bellies with pegs and the necks were cut away as in the pedal harp. The large ones (Plate 35) were about the same size as the old high-headed harps and the superstructure was basically the same shape, though their smooth and rounded outlines seem effeminate compared with the old rugged harp profiles. The strings were of thin brass, with a few of steel in the highest register. A number of these instruments survive in good condition and they can only be described as nightmare parodies of the old Irish harp. Their tone is peculiarly unattractive, rather like that of an ancient and decrepit piano, and the sound is excessively long-lasting unless damped.

The second kind, which Egan marketed as a 'Portable Harp' (Plate 36), was more successful though just as far from the traditional instrument. About three feet (92 cm.) high, its superstructure was more or less the same shape as in the bigger harp, but it was gut-strung and had a mechanism, based on that of the pedal harp, for changing the string lengths to give chromatic notes. Where this was operated in the French harp by means of pedals, it was effected in Egan's small harp by thumb levers set in the forepillar. The instrument was in effect a small single-action 'handle' harp. Tom Moore used one of these to accompany himself when singing his 'Irish Melodies' (to much simpler settings than those published for the piano) and his harp is preserved in the Royal Irish Academy. Similar small instruments were also made in England about the middle of the nineteenth century.

Although the Egan portable harp proved in the end no more than a passing fashion, it was a comparable kind of instrument which eventually became known as the Irish harp in the twentieth century. There seems to have been little harp-playing in Ireland,

PLATE 35. *Harp by Francis Hewson. 1849*

PLATE 36. *Harp by John Egan. 1819*

apart from the visits of foreign virtuosi on the pedal harp, after
the third decade of the nineteenth century. Social conditions
throughout the country were largely deplorable and Irish energies
were directed towards other and more fundamental pursuits. At
the end of the century enthusiasts like James MacFall produced
instruments such as the 'Tara Harp', made in 1902 for Cardinal
Logue. This had a box like a pedal harp set on three little feet, a
slim, curved forepillar with a T-formation copied from the
medieval low-headed Irish harp, a high head and elaborate decoration—in all, a charming piece of antiquarian *art nouveau*.

The traditional harps and harping styles were indeed gone, but
during the nineteenth century a number of devoted men, including
Henry Hudson, George Petrie assisted by Eugene O'Curry, James
Goodman and Patrick Joyce, collected and noted down a great
quantity of Irish music, both words and tunes. Such Irish music as
was commercially published (a considerable amount was issued in
London) was arranged in the harmonic idiom and pianistic style
of the times. The situation is different, however, in the twentieth
century. There is greater knowledge of national and traditional
music in its own context and in many countries there are government subsidies to preserve and study it and to present it in valid
terms to the general public. Inflated and over-romantic presentation
is less acceptable nowadays. In Ireland and among people of Irish
origin elsewhere, the small harp has come to be used to accompany
the concert performance of Irish folk song, much as the guitar is
used elsewhere, and instruments are now made in Ireland, Scotland,
England, the United States of America and even Japan.

Unlike the harps of medieval Ireland, they are not standardized
(Plates 37 and 38). Some makers still follow the general shape of
the superstructure of Egan's small harps; others, particularly in
Ireland and Scotland, use something closer to the outline of the
traditional Irish low-headed harp. All, however, have a pedal-harp
kind of soundbox with a flat belly and rounded or occasionally
ribbed back, and all are strung with gut or nylon. They have simple
apparatus for changing individual string-lengths based on the
seventeenth-century German hand-turned hook principle which
preceded the invention of the pedal-operated string-shortening
mechanism. This means that the small harp can be quickly set in a
different key from that in which it is originally tuned and selected
notes can be further changed while playing, provided the texture of

PLATE 37. *Harp by J. W. Briggs of Glasgow. 1938*

PLATE 38. *Harp by Daniel Quinn of Dublin*

the music allows the left hand to be free momentarily to turn the appropriate blade.

The technique of playing is largely derived from that of the pedal harp. Nothing comparable with the vigorous technique and vivacious repertoire of the Latin-American harpists, most of whom play what is essentially a Spanish seventeenth-century type of harp, has yet developed. Some Irish composers, however, including Brian Boydell and Seoirse Bodley, are writing songs, solos and ensemble music for the small harp, and a comprehensive tutor and companion, *The Irish Harp Book*, by Sheila Larchet Cuthbert, was published in 1975.

A few players, notably Mary Rowland and Osian Ellis, have experimented with the old fingernail technique and use it to great effect. The modern Irish harp played with fingernails is often used in contemporary performances of medieval music. Different as it is from its historic predecessor, it has a justifiable place in the re-creation for twentiety-century audiences of music from the time when the old Irish harp, with its willow soundbox and brass strings, was in its heyday.

Neo-Irish harps of various kinds are often used, generally in combination with other instruments, both acoustic and electronic, by Irish folk and/or rock groups such as The Chieftains and Clannad, and by groups of non-Irish origin who perform 'pan-Celtic' repertory.

Index of Extant Irish Harps

BALLINDERRY FRAGMENTS
Decorated bronze fittings from a large low-headed harp. Boss from neck finial, brace from neck-to-forepillar joint, neck bands with 36 pin-holes, 31 surviving pins—19 of forged bronze, 12 of cast bronze.

16th century. National Museum of Ireland, Dublin. PLATES 17, 18

BUNWORTH HARP
Large high-headed harp with carved, incised and painted decoration, made for the Reverend John Bunworth by John Kelly. One-piece soundbox; narrow brass strip along centre of box with perforated string-holes; 36 strings; 36 brass pins.

1734. Museum of Fine Art, Boston, Massachusetts, U.S.A. PLATE 30

CAROLAN HARP
Large high-headed harp, said to have belonged to Carolan. Forepillar, neck and one-piece soundbox of sycamore; alternately brass shoes and perforated triangular brass plates round string-holes; 35 strings; 35 brass pins of which some appear to be replacements.

Late 17th or early 18th century. National Museum of Ireland, Dublin. PLATES 31, 32

DALWAY FRAGMENTS
Neck and most of forepillar of a large low-headed harp made by Donnchadh mac Tadgh for Sir John Fitzgerald of Cloyne. Neck of yew, forepillar of spindle-wood, elaborately carved with motifs, animals, the Fitzgerald arms and inscriptions in Latin and Irish reading:
Latin: *Bravery flourishes by wounds. Press Forward.* (mottoes of the coats of arms).
I.G.E. and E.B. caused me to be made. I am the queen of harps. I sound, I conquer. I rule . . . [animals] men. Music consoles the troubled mind just as the sound . . . Thus passes worldly pomp. Truth conquers. Donatus the son of Thade made me. My hope [is] in God.
Irish: *The following were the members of the household staff of John Fitzedmond Fitzgerald at Cloyne at the time that I was made: James Fitzjohn was Wine Butler, John Ruane was Beer Butler, and Philip MacDonnell was Cook, in the year 1621. Thade Ó Rourke was Chamberlain and James Russell was Major Domo, and there were also*

75

Maurice Fitzthomas and Maurice Fitzedmund; these were all trusted retainers. Philip the son of Thade McGrath was Tailor. Donough sone of Thade was Carpenter [and the craftsman] who made me. My Musician and Minstrel was Giolláphadraig Mac Críodáin, and none better could I have had, together with Diarmaid Mac Críodáin—two masters [of music] who [fostered and] trained me. And on each and every one of these may God have mercy.

45 pin-holes in neck plus 7 in secondary rank; 42 surviving pins.

1621. National Museum of Ireland, Dublin. PLATE 20

DOWNHILL HARP

Large low-headed harp with some high-headed features, made by Cormac Kelly and played for many years by Denis Hempson. Forepillar, neck and one-piece soundbox of alder; six hexafoil pierced soundholes; 32 string-holes in box, surrounded by perforated triangular brass plates; 30 pin-holes in neck; 27 surviving pins, some brass and some bronze; inscribed on side of soundbox:

*In the time of Noah I was green
Since his flood I had not been seen
Until seventeen hundred and two I was found
By Cormac O Kelly underground
He raised me up to that degree
The Queen of Musicke you may call me*

1702. Messrs. Arthur Guinness, Son and Co., Dublin. PLATES 33, 34

FITZGERALD-KILDARE HARP

Large low-headed harp elegantly decorated with carved scrolls, birds, animal and human heads, the arms and crest of the Fitzgerald family and the inscription *RFG fecit Anno 1275* (the second figure is uncertain). Forepillar of birch, neck of pear, one-piece soundbox of willow; two rectangle-and-quatrefoil pierced soundholes; 38 string-holes in box, with brass shoes; 36 pin-holes in neck; 36 brass pins.

Late 16th or 17th century. National Museum of Ireland, Dublin. PLATES 23, 24

LAMONT HARP

Small low-headed harp with brass neck finial boss and two neck-to-forepillar braces. Forepillar, neck and one-piece soundbox of hornbeam; four soundholes; 32 string-holes in box; the three highest and two lowest with brass shoes, the rest with perforated triangular brass plates (possibly replacements); 30 pin-holes in neck; 30 surviving pins of which some are replacements.

15th century. National Museum of Antiquities of Scotland, Edinburgh. PLATE 13

MULLAGH MAST HARP

Large high-headed harp. Forepillar, neck and one-piece soundbox of willow; box covered with roughly incised trellis, spirals and circles; 33 string-holes in box, the nine lowest surrounded by overlapping perforated reversed triangles of copper, a few of the rest with brass shoes of which the remainder are missing; 33 pin-holes in neck; no surviving pins.

Early 18th century. National Museum of Ireland, Dublin. PLATE 28

O FFOGERTY HARP
Large low-headed harp. Forepillar, neck and one-piece soundbox of willow; six soundholes; 36 string-holes with brass shoes; 36 pin-holes in neck; 35 surviving brass pins.

17th century. Captain Ryan. PLATE 22

O'NEILL HARP
Large high-headed harp with painted decoration. One-piece sound-box with narrow brass strip along centre with 39 perforations for strings; 36 brass pins. (There is no evidence that this harp belonged to Arthur O'Neill).

18th century. Ulster Museum, Belfast. PLATE 29

OTWAY HARP
Large low-headed harp with carved and incised decoration. One-piece soundbox with four hexafoil pierced soundholes; 35 string-holes; shoes missing; originally 34 pin-holes in neck; 9 surviving brass pins.

17th century. Captain R. J. O. Otway-Ruthven, D.S.O., R.N. PLATE 21

QUEEN MARY HARP
Small low-headed harp with carved and incised decoration. Forepillar, neck and one-piece soundbox of hornbeam; 4 soundholes; 29 string-holes with brass shoes above and brass strips below all but the highest 6; wooden pegs added, probably, in the nineteenth century; 29 pin-holes in neck; 29 pins, some brass some iron; additional string-hole below metal band in neck and iron loop set in bottom of forepillar not original.

c. 1500. National Museum of Antiquities of Scotland. PLATE 12

SIRR HARP
Large high-headed harp with eagle's head and rodent's head carved on neck. Forepillar of alder, neck and one-piece soundbox of willow; 4 soundholes; narrow brass strip up centre of box with 36 perforations for strings plus two at the top and four at the bottom which are superfluous and not drilled to size; 36 pin-holes and bridge pins in neck; 35 surviving iron pins.

18th century. National Museum of Ireland, Dublin. PLATES 26, 27

TRINITY COLLEGE DUBLIN HARP
Small low-headed harp with carved and incised decoration, silver

neck finial boss and neck bands. Forepillar, neck and one-piece sound-box of willow; 4 soundholes; 30 string-holes (the lowest covered by reconstruction of base of forepillar) with brass shoes; 29 pin-holes in neck; 29 silver pins.

14th century. Trinity College, Dublin. PLATE 11

Acknowledgements

Plates 1, 2, 10. By courtesy of the Trustees of the British Museum, London.

3. By courtesy of Stiftsbibliothek, St. Gall, Switzerland.

4. By courtesy of Mr. David Boath Thoms.

5, 6, 7, 8. By courtesy of the National Monuments Branch of the Office of Public Works, Dublin.

9, 15, 17, 18, 20, 21, 23, 24, 26, 27, 28, 31, 32, 35. By courtesy of the National Museum of Ireland, Dublin.

11. By courtesy of the Provost of Trinity College, Dublin; photograph by courtesy of the Trustees of the British Museum, London.

12, 13. By courtesy of the National Museum of Antiquities of Scotland, Edinburgh.

14. By courtesy of An Dr Caoimhín Ó Danachair.

21. By courtesy of Captain R. J. O. Otway-Ruthven, D.S.O., R.N.; photograph by courtesy of John Pierse, Horsham.

25. By kind permission of the Governing Body of Christ Church, Oxford.

29. By courtesy of the Director, the Ulster Museum, Belfast.

33, 34. By courtesy of Messrs. Arthur Guinness, Son and Co., Dublin; photograph by courtesy of the National Museum of Ireland.

36. By courtesy of the Metropolitan Museum of Art, The Crosby Brown Collection of Musical Instruments, 1889, New York, U.S.A.

37. By courtesy of Mrs. Mary Rowland; photograph by Garth Dawson, Accrington.

38. By courtesy of Mr. Daniel Quinn; photograph by courtesy of the National Museum of Ireland.

SAOL AGUS CULTÚR IN ÉIRINN/IRISH LIFE AND CULTURE

The following booklets have been published in this series: